DATE	ISSUED TO
AUG 2 3 2006	

Care Bears™

Most Valuable Bear

By Justin Spelvin
Illustrated by Jay Johnson

Designed by Rick DeMonico

ISBN 0-439-66958-8

12 11 10 9 8 7 6 5 4 3 2   4 5 6 7 8/0

Printed in the U.S.A.
First printing, September 2004

SCHOLASTIC INC.   **1018260**

New York   Toronto   London   Auckland   Sydney
Mexico City   New Delhi   Hong Kong   Buenos Aires

Champ Bear woke up
bright and early.

It was the perfect day
to do something special.

"Let's play baseball!"
he said to his friends.

"That's a great idea!"
said Good Luck Bear.

"But what if I can't play,"
worried Grumpy Bear.

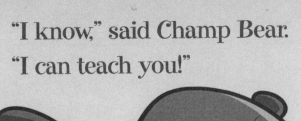

"I know," said Champ Bear.
"I can teach you!"

"First, you pitch the ball,"
said Champ Bear.

He threw fast and straight.
"Wow!" said Good Luck Bear.

"Next, you hit the ball,"
added Champ Bear.

He swung his bat and hit.
The ball flew far and away.
"Can I try?" asked Cheer Bear.

But Champ Bear was not done.
"Then you have to run
around the bases," he said.

"I could do that," said Grumpy Bear.

"You also have to catch,"
said Champ Bear.
He threw a ball in the air
and then caught it.

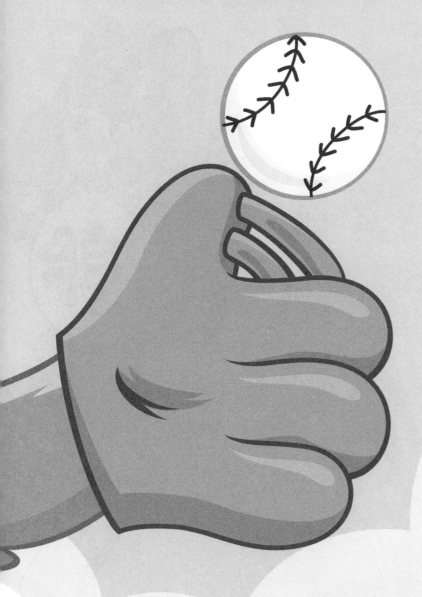

"We're ready to play,"
Good Luck Bear said.
"I want to swing the bat,"
Cheer Bear said.

"I bet I could catch,"
Wish Bear said.

But Champ Bear didn't hear
any of his friends.

Champ Bear was still pitching,
hitting, running, and catching.

So his friends just sat
and watched.

"Playing baseball is not much fun," said Grumpy Bear.

Champ Bear finally stopped.
"I sure am tired," he said.
"Why do you look so sad?"

"You're a great teacher,"
said Cheer Bear.
"But you were so busy
showing us how to play..."

"That none of us got to try,"
Grumpy Bear added.

Share Bear knew what to do.
"If we played as a team,
we could share the fun!"

"And you wouldn't be so tired,"
added Good Luck Bear.

And that's just what they did.
For the rest of the day
they threw, hit, ran,
and caught as a team.

"Thanks for a great game!"
cheered the Care Bears.